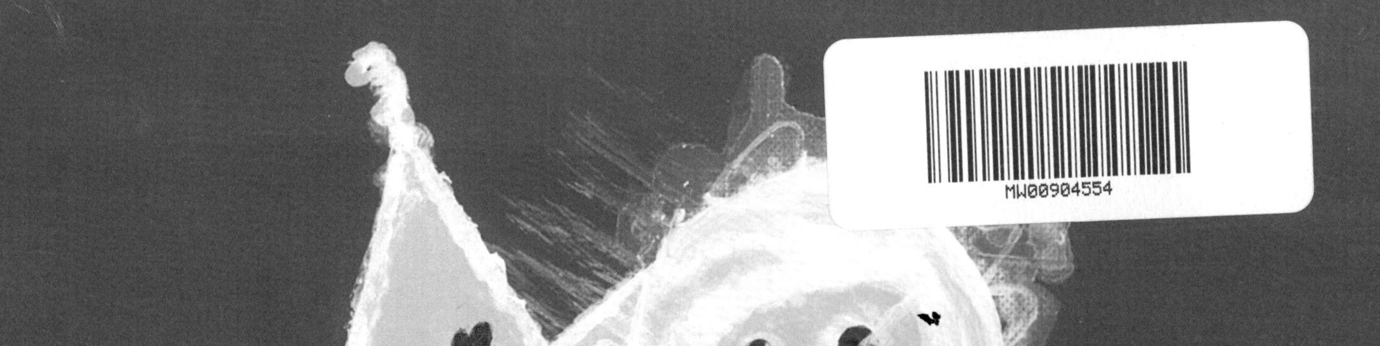

ARE YOU THE NEXT FAMOUS YOUNG AUTHOR

BOO
and the Christmas Star

J. Katyn

I dedicate this book to my daughter Jenn and my son Jonathan and to all children who are inspired to draw pictures and write stories.

Order this book online at www.trafford.com
or email orders@trafford.com

Most Trafford titles are also available at major online book retailers.

Printed in the United States of America.

ISBN: 978-1-4669-9305-1 (sc)

Library of Congress Control Number: 2013907976

Trafford rev. 05/07/2013

www.trafford.com

North America & international
toll-free: 1 888 232 4444 (USA & Canada)
phone: 250 383 6864 • fax: 812 355 4082

Boo and the Christmas Star

There are green creatures in my head trying to get out,

There are also many stars in here, I wonder what they're about?

I keep my pencil, paper, brush and paint close by my bed,

So that in the morning I can make a story about what's in my head.

My name is Boo, I've made a story for you.

I hope you like it!

Oh Christmas tree, oh Christmas tree, thank you
for your many lights. Hey green creatures, what
are you doing?

The stars and the moon have fun together making Christmas bright. Hey green creature, are you planning to throw that moon beam?

The fire department had to be called. I wonder who caused the fire?

Everyone is getting ready for Christmas. I have many Halloween friends, but I would like a Christmas friend. Can the green creatures be my friends?

As I fly through the cloudy sky I see a magnificent sight. What is it? What is that green creature doing?

Wow! It is a star nursery. Every newborn star has a special glow, but one star is just a little more special. Gee, are you green creatures still here? Okay, one of you looks suspicious. What are you doing?

Hey kids, do you like drawing pictures and writing stories? You could become the next famous young author. To become an author you must practice drawing and writing stories. Remember, at first you draw a picture and write a sentence about it. As you get better, you then write your story first and draw a picture for each special part of your story. Also, as you read this story and others, you begin to see how the author did it. Don't forget the author has to draw the front and back cover of the book too.

I think I still miss Halloween. Which of my friends are not in the picture?

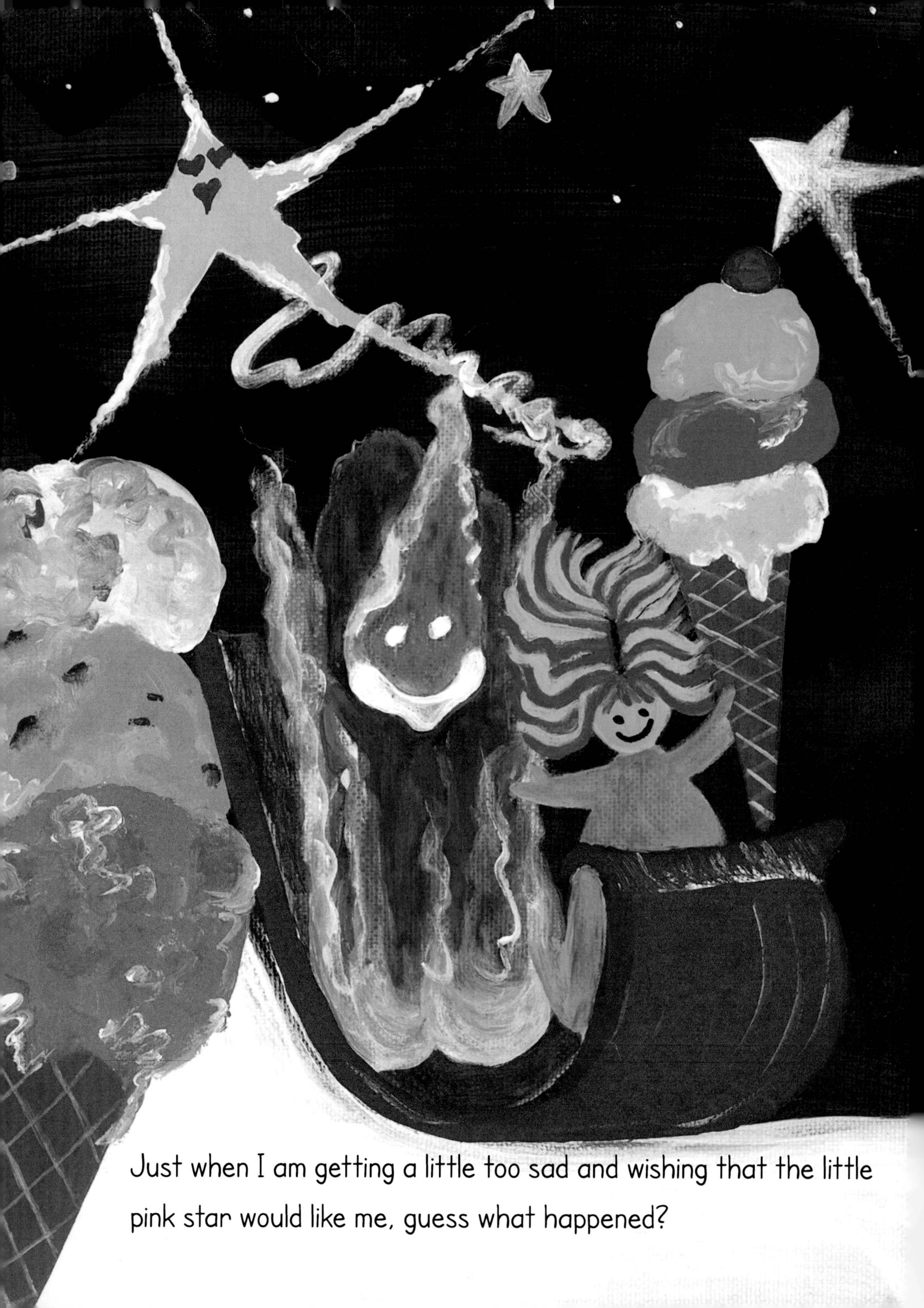

Just when I am getting a little too sad and wishing that the little pink star would like me, guess what happened?

You guessed correctly. The little pink star kissed me and knocked me down the Milky Way star cluster. There is something scary in this picture, what is it?

The little pink star glowed brightly as we met some snowflakes. Making a snow fort is fun, but soon those green creatures returned. Do you like the green creatures?

Boys and girls, how do you like my story so far? Remember you too can draw and colour and write stories. You can make a book just like I did.

As Christmas was soon to arrive, I decided to read one of my other stories to my new friend. Now she wants to make a book of her own.

Gee, Christmas Eve has arrived. My little star friend and I follow Santa and make the night sky shine brightly. Look at Santa! He has everything under control.

I say goodbye to my new star friend and make a special wish. I wish that all the girls and boys have a merry Christmas and a happy Boo night.

-The end-

Edwards Brothers Malloy
Oxnard, CA USA
June 12, 2013